J. D. SALINGER

Three early stories

DEVAULT-GRAVES
DIGITAL EDITIONS
www.devault-gravesagency.com

Cover design: Martina Voriskova
Title page design: Martina Voriskova
Illustrations: Anna Rose Yoken
Page Layout: Patrick Alley

Devault-Graves Digital Editions is an imprint of
The Devault-Graves Agency, LLC
Memphis, Tennessee.
The names Devault-Graves Digital Editions, Lasso Books,
and Chalk Line Books are all imprints and trademarks of
The Devault-Graves Agency.
www.devault-gravesagency.com

Table of Contents

The Young Folks

ABOUT ELEVEN O'CLOCK, Lucille Henderson, observing that her party was soaring at the proper height, and just having been smiled at by Jack Delroy, forced herself to glance over in the direction of Edna Phillips, who since eight o'clock had been sitting in the big red chair, smoking cigarettes and yodeling hellos and wearing a very bright eye which young men were not bothering to catch. Edna's direction still the same, Lucille Henderson sighed as heavily as her dress would allow, and then, knitting what there was of her brows, gazed about the room at the noisy young people she had invited to drink up her father's scotch. Then abruptly, she swished to where William Jameson Junior sat, biting his fingernails and staring at the small blonde girl sitting on the floor with three young men from Rutgers.

"Hello there," Lucille Henderson said, clutching William Jameson Junior's arm. "Come on," she said. "There's someone I'd like you to meet."

"Who?"

"This girl. She's swell." And Jameson followed her across the room, at the same time trying to make short work of a hangnail on his thumb.

"Edna baby," Lucille Henderson said, "I'd love you to really

know Bill Jameson. Bill—Edna Phillips. Or have you two birds met already?"

"No," said Edna, taking in Jameson's large nose, flabby mouth, narrow shoulders. "I'm awfully glad to meet you," she told him.

"Gladda know ya," Jameson replied, mentally contrasting Edna's all with the all of the small blonde across the room.

"Bill's a very good friend of Jack Delroy's," Lucille reported.

"I don't know him so good," said Jameson.

"Well. I gotta beat it. See ya later, you two!"

"Take it easy!" Edna called after her. Then, "Won't you sit down?"

"Well, I don't know," Jameson said. "I been sitting down all night, kinda."

"I didn't know you were a good friend of Jack Delroy's," Edna said. "He's a grand person, don't you think?"

"Yeah, he's alright, I guess. I don't know him so good. I never went around with his crowd much."

"Oh, really? I thought I heard Lu say you were a good friend of his."

"Yeah, she did. Only I don't know him so good. I really oughtta be gettin' home. I got this theme for Monday I'm supposed to do. I wasn't really gonna come home this weekend."

"Oh, but the party's young!" Edna said. "The shank of the

evening!"

"The what?"

"The shank of the evening. I mean it's so early yet."

"Yeah," said Jameson. "But I wasn't even gonna come t'night. Accounta this theme. Honest. I wasn't gonna come home this weekend at all."

"But it's so early I mean!" Edna said.

"Yeah, I know, but—"

"What's your theme on, anyway?"

Suddenly, from the other side of the room, the small blonde shrieked with laughter, the three young men from Rutgers anxiously joined her.

"I say what's your theme on, anyway?" Edna repeated.

"Oh, I don't know," Jameson said. "About this description of some cathedral. This cathedral in Europe. I don't know."

"Well, I mean what do you have to do?"

"I don't know. I'm supposed to criticize it, sort of. I got it written down."

Again the small blonde and her friends went off into high laughter.

"Criticize it? Oh, then you've seen it?"

"Seen what?" said Jameson.

"This cathedral."

"Me? Hell, no."

"Well, I mean how can you criticize it if you've never seen it?"

"Oh. Yeah. It's not me. It's this guy that wrote it. I'm supposed to criticize it from what he wrote, kinda."

"Mmm. I see. That sounds *hard*."

"Wudga say?"

"I say that sounds hard. I know. I've wrestled with that stuff puhlenty myself."

"Yeah."

"Who's the rat that wrote it?" Edna said.

Exuberance again from the locale of the small blonde.

"What?" Jameson said.

"I say who wrote it?"

"I don't know. John Ruskin."

"Oh, boy," Edna said. "You're in for it fella."

"Wudga say?"

"I say you're in for it. I mean that stuff's hard."

"Oh. Yeah. I guess so."

Edna said, "Who're ya looking at? I know most of the gang here tonight."

"Me?" Jameson said. "Nobody. I think maybe I'll get a drink."

"Hey! You took the words right out of my mouth."

They arose simultaneously. Edna was taller than Jameson and Jameson was shorter than Edna.

"I think," Edna said, "there's some stuff out there on the terrace. Some kind of junk, anyway. Not sure. We can try.

Might as well get a breath of fresh air."

"All right," said Jameson.

They moved on toward the terrace, Edna crouching slightly and brushing off imaginary ashes from what had been her lap since eight o'clock. Jameson followed her, looking behind him and gnawing on the index finger of his left hand.

For reading, sewing, mastering crossword puzzles, the Henderson terrace was inadequately lighted. Lightly charging through the screen door, Edna was almost immediately aware of hushed vocal tones coming from a much darker vicinity to her left. But she walked directly to the front of the terrace, leaned heavily on the white railing, took a very deep breath, and then turned and looked behind her for Jameson.

"I hear somebody talkin'," Jameson said, joining her.

"Shhh....Isn't it a gorgeous night? Just take a deep breath."

"Yeah. Where's the stuff? The scotch?"

"Just a second," Edna said. "Take a deep breath. Just once."

"Yeah, I did. Maybe that's it over there." He left her and went over to a table. Edna turned and watched him. By silhouette mostly, she saw him lift and set things on the table.

"Nothing left!" Jameson called back.

"*Shhh*. Not so loud. C'mere a minute."

He went over to her.

"What's the matter?" he asked.

"Just look at that sky," Edna said.

"Yeah. I can hear somebody talkin' over there, can't you?"

"Yes, you ninny."

"Wuddaya mean *ninny*?"

"*Some* people," Edna said, "wanna be *alone*."

"Oh. Yeah. I get it."

"Not so *loud*. How would you like it if someone spoiled it for you?"

"Yeah. Sure," Jameson said.

"I think I'd kill somebody, wouldn't you?"

"I don't know. Yeah. I guess so."

"What do you do most of the time when you're home weekends, anyway? Edna asked.

"Me? I don't know."

"Sow the old wild oats, I guess, huh?"

"I don't getcha," Jameson said.

"You know. Chase around. Joe College stuff."

"Naa. I don't know. Not much."

"You know something," Edna said abruptly, "you remind me a lot of this boy I used to go around with last summer. I mean the way you look and all. And Barry was your build almost exactly. You know. Wiry."

"Yeah?"

"Mmm. He was an artist. Oh, Lord!"

"What's the matter?"

"Nothing. Only I'll never forget this time he wanted to do a portrait of me. He used to always say to me—serious as the devil, too—'Eddie, you're not beautiful according to conventional standards, but there's something in your face I wanna catch.' Serious as the devil he'd say it, I mean. Well. I only posed for him this once."

"Yeah," said Jameson. "Hey, I could go in and bring out some stuff—"

"No," Edna said, "let's just have a cigarette. It's so grand out here. Amorous voices and all, what?"

"I don't think I got any more with me. I got some in the other room, I think."

"No, don't bother," Edna told him. "I have some right here." She opened her evening bag and brought out a small black, rhinestoned case, opened it, and offered one of three cigarettes to Jameson. Taking one, Jameson remarked that he really oughtta get going, that he had told her about this theme he had for Monday. He finally found his matches, and struck a light.

"Oh," Edna said, puffing on her cigarette, "it'll be breaking up pretty soon. Did you notice Doris Leggett, by the way?"

"Which one is she?"

"Terribly short? Rather blonde? Used to go with Pete

Ilesner? Oh, you must have seen her. She was sitting on the floor per usual, laughing at the top of her voice."

"That her? You know her?" Jameson said.

"Well, sort of," Edna told him. "We never went around much together. I really know her mostly by what Pete Ilesner used to tell me."

"Who's he?"

"Petie Ilesner? Don't you know Petie? Oh, he's a *grand* guy. He went around with Doris Leggett for a while. And in my opinion she gave him a pretty raw deal. Simply rotten, *I* think."

"How?" Jameson said. "Wuddaya mean?"

"Oh, let's drop it. You know me. I hate to put my two cents in when I'm not sure and all. Not any more. Only I *don't* think Petie would lie to me though. After all, I mean."

"She's not bad," said Jameson. "Doris Liggett?"

"Leggett," Edna said. "I guess Doris *is* attractive to men. I don't know. I think I really liked her better though—her looks, I mean—when her hair was natural. I mean bleached hair—to me anyway—always looks sort of artificial when you see it in the light or something. I don't know. I may be wrong. Every-body does it, I guess. Lord! I'll bet Dad would *kill* me if I ever came home with my hair touched up even a *little*! You don't know Dad. He's terribly old fashioned. I honestly don't think I ever *would* have it touched up, when

you come right *down* to it. But you know. Sometimes you do the craziest things. Lord! Dad's not the only one! I think *Barry* even would kill me if I ever did!"

"Who?" said Jameson.

"Barry. This boy I told you about."

"He here t'night?"

"*Barry*? Lord, no! I can just picture Barry at one of these things. You don't know *Barry*."

"Go t'college?"

"Barry? Mmm, he did. Princeton. I *think* Barry got out in thirty-four. Not sure. I really haven't seen Barry since last summer. Well, not to talk to. Parties and stuff. I always managed to look the other way when *he* looked at *me*. Or ran out to the john or something."

"I thought you liked him, this guy," Jameson said.

"Mmm. I did. Up to a point."

"I don't getcha."

"Let it go. I'd rather not talk about it. He just asked too much of me; that's all."

"Oh," said Jameson.

"I'm not a prude or anything. I don't know. Maybe I am. I just have my own standards and in my funny little way I try to live up to them. The best I can, anyway."

"Look," Jameson said. "This railing is kinda shaky—"

Edna said, "It isn't that I can't appreciate how a boy feels

after he dates you all summer and spends money he hasn't any right to spend on theater tickets and night spots and all. I mean, I can understand. He feels you owe him something. Well, I'm not that way. I guess I'm just not built that way. It's gotta be the real thing with me. Before, you know. I mean, love and all."

"Yeah. Look, uh. I really oughtta get goin'. I got this theme for Monday. Hell, I shoulda been home hours ago. So I think I'll go in and get a drink and get goin'."

"Yes," Edna said. "Go on in."

"Aren'tcha coming?"

"In a minute. Go ahead."

"Well. See ya," Jameson said.

Edna shifted her position at the railing. She lighted the remaining cigarette in her case. Inside, somebody had turned on the radio, or the volume suddenly had increased. A girl vocalist was huskying through the refrain from that new show, which even the delivery boys were beginning to whistle.

No door slams like a screen door.

"Edna!" Lucille Henderson greeted.

"Hey, hey," said Edna. "Hello Harry."

"Wuttaya say."

"Bill's inside," Lucille said. "Get me a drink, willya, Harry?"

"Sure."

"What happened?" Lucille wanted to know. "Didn't you and Bill hit it off? Is that Frances and Eddie over there?"

"I don't know. He hadda leave. He had a lot of work to do for Monday."

"Well, right now he's in there on the floor with Dottie Leggett. Delroy's putting peanuts down her back. That is Frances and Eddie over there."

"Your little Bill is quite a guy."

"Yeah? How? Wuttaya mean?" said Lucille.

Edna fish-lipped her mouth and tapped her cigarette ashes.

"A trifle *warm*-blooded, shall I say?"

"Bill *Jameson*?"

"Well," said Edna, "I'm still in one piece. Only keep that guy away from me, willya?"

"Hmm. Live and learn," said Lucille Henderson. "Where is that dope Harry? I'll see ya later, Ed."

When she finished her cigarette, Edna went in too. She walked quickly, directly up the stairs into the section of Lucille Henderson's mother's home barred to young hands holding lighted cigarettes and wet highball glasses. She remained upstairs nearly twenty minutes. When she came down, she went back into the living room. William Jameson Junior, a glass in his right hand and the fingers of his left hand in or close to his mouth, was sitting a few men away

from the small blonde. Edna sat down in the big red chair. No one had taken it. She opened her evening bag and took out her small black, rhinestoned case, and extracted one of ten or twelve cigarettes.

"Hey!" she called, tapping her cigarette on the arm of the big red chair. "Hey, Lu! Bobby! See if you can't get something better on the radio! I mean *who* can dance to that stuff?"

Go See Eddie

HELEN'S BEDROOM WAS always straightened while she bathed so that when she came out of the bathroom her dressing table was free of last night's cream jars and soiled tissues, and there were glimpses in her mirror of flat bed-spreads and patted chair cushions. When it was sunny, as it was now, there were bright warm blotches to bring out the pastels chosen from the decorator's little book.

She was brushing her thick red hair when Elsie, the maid, came in.

"Mr. Bobby's here, ma'am," said Elsie.

"Bobby?" asked Helen. "I thought he was in Chicago. Hand me my robe, Elsie. Then show him in."

Arranging her royal-blue robe to cover her long bare legs, Helen went on brushing her hair. Then abruptly a tall sandy-haired man in a polo coat brushed behind and past her, snapping his index finger against the back of her neck. He walked directly to the chaise-lounge on the other side of the room and stretched himself out, coat and all. Helen could see him in her mirror.

"Hello, you," she said. "Hey. That thing was just straight-ened. I thought you were in Chicago."

"Got back last night," Bobby said, yawning. "God, I'm tired."

"Successful?" asked Helen. "Didn't you go to hear some girl sing or something?"

"Uh," Bobby affirmed.

"Was she any good, the girl?"

"Lot of breast-work. No voice."

Helen set down her brush, got up, and seated herself in the peach-colored straight chair at Bobby's feet. From her robe pocket she took an emery board and proceeded to apply it to her long, flesh-pink nails. "What else do you know?" she inquired.

"Not much," said Bobby. He sat up with a grunt, took a package of cigarettes from his overcoat pocket, stuck them back, then stood up to remove the overcoat. He tossed the heavy thing on Helen's bed, scattering a colony of sunbeams. Helen continued filing her nails. Bobby sat on the edge of the chaise-lounge, lighted a cigarette, and leaned forward. The sun was on them both, lushing her milky skin, and doing nothing for Bobby but showing up his dandruff and the pockets under his eyes.

"How would you like a job?" Bobby asked.

"A job?" Helen said, filing. "What kind of job?"

"Eddie Jackson's going into rehearsals with a new show. I saw him last night. You oughtta see how gray that guy's getting. I said to him, have you got a spot for my sister? He said maybe, and I told him you might be around."

"It's a good thing you said *might*," Helen said, looking up at him. "What kind of a spot? Third from the left or something?"

"I didn't ask him what kind of a spot. But it's better than nothing, isn't it?"

Helen didn't answer him, went on attending to her nails.

"Why don't you want a job?"

"I didn't say I didn't want one."

"Well, then what's the matter with seeing Jackson?"

"I don't want anymore chorus work. Besides, I hate Eddie Jackson's guts."

"Yeah," said Bobby. He got up and went to the door. "Elsie!" he called. "Bring me a cup of coffee!" Then he sat down again.

"I want you to see Eddie," he told her.

"I don't want to see Eddie."

"I want you to see him. Put down that goddam file a minute."

She went on filing.

"I want you to go up there this afternoon, hear?"

"I'm not going up there this afternoon or any other afternoon," Helen told him, crossing her legs. "Who do you think you're ordering around?"

Bobby's hand was half fist when he knocked the emery board from her fingers. She neither looked at him nor

picked up the emery board from the carpet. She just got up and went back to her dressing table to resume brushing her hair, her thick red hair. Bobby followed to stand behind her, to look for her eyes in the mirror.

"I want you to see Eddie this afternoon. Hear me, Helen?" Helen brushed her hair. "And what'll you do if I don't go up there, tough guy?"

He picked that up. "Would you like me to tell you? Would you like me to tell you what I'll do if you don't go up there?"

"Yes, I'd like you to tell me what you'll do if I don't go up there," Helen mimicked.

"Don't do that. I'll push in that glamour kisser of yours. So help me," Bobby warned. "I want you to go up there. I want you see Eddie and I want you to take that goddam job."

"No, I want you to tell me what you'll do if I don't go there," Helen said, but in her natural voice.

"I'll tell you what I'll do," Bobby said, watching her eyes in the mirror. "I'll ring up your greasy boyfriend's wife and tell her what's what."

Helen horse-laughed. "Go ahead!" she told him. "Go right ahead, wise guy! She knows *all* about it!"

Bobby said, "She knows, eh?"

"Yes, she knows! And don't you call Phil greasy! You wish you were half as good looking as he is!"

"He's a greaser. A greasy lousy cheat," Bobby pronounced.

"Two for a lousy dime. That's your boyfriend."

"Coming from you that's good."

"Have you ever seen his wife?" Bobby asked.

"Yes-I've-seen-his-wife. What about her?"

"Have you seen her face?"

"What's so marvelous about her face?"

"Nothing's so marvelous about it! She hasn't got a glamour kisser like yours. It's just a nice face. Why the hell don't you leave her dumb husband alone?"

"None of your business why!" snapped Helen.

The fingers of his right hand suddenly dug into the hollow of her shoulder. She yelled out in pain, turned, and from an awkward position but with all her might, slammed his hand with the flat of her hairbrush. He sucked in his breath, pivoted swiftly so that his back was both to Helen and to Elsie, the maid, who had come in with his coffee. Elsie set the tray on the window seat next to the chair where Helen had filed her nails, then slipped out of the room.

Bobby sat down, and with the use of his other hand, sipped his coffee black. Helen, at the dressing table, had begun to place her hair. She wore it in a heavy old-fashioned bun.

He had long finished his coffee when the last hairpin was in its place. Then she went over to where he sat smoking and looking out the window. Drawing the lapels of her robe

closer to her breast, she sat down with a little *oop* sound of unbalance on the floor at his feet. She placed a hand on his ankle, stroked it, and addressed him in a different voice.

"Bobby, I'm sorry. But you made me lose my temper, darling. Did I hurt your hand?"

"Never mind my hand," he said, keeping it in his pocket.

"Bobby, I love Phil. On my word of honor. I don't want you to think I'm just playing around. You don't, do you? I mean you don't just think I'm playing around, trying to hurt people?"

Bobby made no reply.

"My word of honor, Bob. You don't know Phil. He's really a grand person."

Bobby looked at her. "You and your goddam grand persons. You know more goddam grand persons. The guy from Cleveland. What the hell was his name? Bothwell. Harry Bothwell. And how 'bout that blond kid used to sing at Bill Cassidy's? Two of the goddamndest grandest persons you ever met." He looked out the window again. "Oh, for Chrissake, Helen," he said finally.

"Bob," said Helen, "you know how old I was. I was terribly young. You know that. But Bob, this is the real thing. Honestly. I know it is. I've never felt this way before. Bob, you don't really in your heart think I'm taking all this from Phil just for the hell of it?"

Bobby looked at her again, lifted his eyebrows, thinned his lips. "You know what I hear in Chicago?" he asked her.

"What, Bob?" Helen asked gently, the tips of her fingers rubbing his ankle.

"I heard two guys talking. You don't know 'em. They were talking about you. You and this horsey-set guy, Hanson Carpenter. They crummied the thing inside out." He paused. "You with him, too, Helen?"

"That's a goddam lie, Bob," Helen told him softly. "Bob, I hardly know Hanson Carpenter well enough to say hello to him."

"Maybe so! But it's a wonderful thing for a brother to have to listen to, isn't it? Everybody in town gives me the horse-laugh when they see me comin' around the corner!"

"Bobby. If you believe that slop it's your own damn fault. What do you care what they say? You're bigger than they are. You don't have to pay any attention to their dirty minds."

"I didn't say I believed it. I said it was what I heard. That's bad enough, isn't it?"

"Well, it's not so," Helen told him. "Toss me a cigarette there, hmm?"

He flipped the package of cigarettes into her lap; then matches. She lighted up, inhaled, and removed a piece of tobacco from her tongue with the tips of her fingers.

"You used to be such a swell kid," Bobby stated briefly.

"Oh! And I ain't no more?" Helen little-girl'd.

He was silent.

"Listen, Helen. I'll tell ya. I had lunch the other day, before I went to Chicago, with Phil's wife."

"Yeah?"

"She's a swell kid. Class," Bobby told her.

"Class, huh?" said Helen.

"Yeah. Listen. Go see Eddie this afternoon. It can't do any harm. Go see him."

Helen smoked. "I hate Eddie Jackson. He always makes a play for me."

"Listen," said Bobby, standing up. "You know how to turn on the ice when you want to." He stood over her. "I have to go. I haven't gone to the office yet."

Helen stood up and watched him put on his polo coat.

"Go see Eddie," Bobby said, putting on his pigskin gloves.

"Hear me?" He buttoned his overcoat. "I'll give you a ring soon."

Helen chided, "Oh, you'll give me a ring soon! When? The fourth of July?"

"No. Soon. I've been busy as hell lately. Where's my hat? Oh, I didn't have one."

She walked with him to the front door, stood in the doorway until the elevator came. Then she shut the door and

walked quickly back to her room. She went to the telephone and dialed swiftly but precisely.

"Hello?" she said into the mouthpiece. "Let me speak to Mr. Stone, please. This is Miss Mason." In a moment his voice came through. "Phil?" she said. "Listen. My brother Bobby was just here. And do you know why? Because that adorable little Vassar-faced wife of yours told him about you and I. Yes! Listen, Phil. Listen to me. I don't like it. I don't care if you had anything to do with it or not. I don't like it. I don't care. No, I can't. I have a previous engagement. I can't tonight either. You can call me tomorrow. I'm very upset about all this. I said you can call me *tomorrow*, Phil. No. I said *no*. Phil. Goodbye."

She set down the receiver, crossed her legs, and bit thoughtfully at the cuticle of her thumb. Then she turned and yelled loudly: "*Elsie!*"

Elsie moused into the room.

"Take away Mr. Bobby's tray."

When Elsie was out of the room, Helen dialed again.

"Hanson?" she said. "This is me. Us. We. You dog."

Once a Week Won't Kill You

HE HAD A cigarette in his mouth while he packed, and his face squinted to avoid smoke in the eyes; so there was no way of telling by his expression whether he was bored or apprehensive, annoyed or resigned. The young woman sitting in the big man's chair, looking like a guest, had her pretty face caught in a blotch of early morning sunshine; it did her no harm. But her arms were probably the best of her. They were brown and round and good.

"Sweetie," she said, "I don't see why Billy couldn't be doing all that. I mean."

"What?" said the young man. He had a thick, chain-smoker's voice.

"I mean I don't see why Billy couldn't be doing all that."

"He's too old," he answered. "How 'bout turning on the radio. There might be some canned music on at this time. Try 1010."

The young woman reached behind her, using the hand with the gold band wedding ring and on the little finger beside it the incredible emerald; she opened some white compartment doors, snapped something, turned something. She sat back and waited, and suddenly, without any pretext, she yawned. The young man glanced at her.

"What a *horrible* time to start, I mean," she said.

"I'll tell them," said the young man, examining a stack of folded handkerchiefs. "My wife says it's a horrible time to start out."

"Sweetie, I *am* going to miss you horribly."

"I'll miss you, too. I have more white handkerchiefs than this."

"I mean, I *will*," she said. "It's all so *stinking*. I mean. And all"

"Well, that's that," said the young man, closing the valise. He lighted a cigarette, looked at the bed, and dropped himself on it....

Just as he stretched himself out the tubes of the radio were warmed, and a Sousa march, featuring what seemed to be an unlimited fife section, triumphed voluminously into the room. His wife swung back one of her marvelous arms and put a stop to it.

"There might have been something else on."

"Not at this *crazy* time."

The young man blew a faulty smoke ring at the ceiling.

"You didn't have to get up," he told her.

"I wanted to."

It had been three years and she had never stopped talking to him in italics.

"Not get *up*!" she said.

"Try 570," he said. "There might be something there."

His wife tried the radio again, and they both waited, he closing his eyes. In a moment some reliable jazz came through.

"Do you have enough *time* to lay down like that? I mean."

"To lie down like that—yes. It's early."

His wife suddenly seemed to be struck with a rather serious conjecture. "I *hope* they put you in the Calvary. The Calvary's lovely," she said. "I'm mad about those little sword do-hickies they wear on their collars. And you *love* to *ride* and all."

"The Cavalry," said the young man, with his eyes shut. "There's not much chance of that stuff. Everybody's going to the Infantry, these days."

"*Horrible*, Sweetie, I *wish* you'd phone that man with the thing on his face. The Colonel. The one at Phyll and Kenny's last week. In Intelligence and all. I mean *you* speak French and *German* and all. He'd certainly get you at *least* a *commission*. I mean you know how *miserable* you'll be just being a private or something. I mean you even hate to *talk* to people and everything."

"Please," he said. "Keep quiet about that. I told you about that. That commission business."

"Well, I hope at *least* they send you to *London*. I mean where there's some *civilized* people. Do you have Bubby's

APO number?"

"Yes," he lied.

His wife was making another apparently grave conjecture. "I'd *love* some material. Some tweed. *Anything.*" Then, almost instantly, she yawned, and said the wrong thing: "Did you say good-by to your aunt?"

Her husband opened his eyes, sat up rather sharply, and swung his feet over to the floor. "Virginia. Listen. I didn't get a chance to finish last night," he said. "I want you to take her to the movies once a week."

"The movies?"

"It won't kill you," he said. "Once a week won't kill you."

"No, of *course* not, Sweetie, but—"

"No buts," he said. "Once a week won't kill you."

"Of *course* I'll take her, you *crazy*. I only meant—"

"It isn't too much to ask. She isn't young or anything any more."

"But, Sweetie, I mean she's getting *worse* again. I mean she's so *batty*, she isn't even *funny*. I mean *you're* not in the *house* with her all day."

"Neither are you," he said. "And besides, she doesn't ever leave her rooms unless I take her out somewhere or something." He leaned closer to her, almost sitting off the edge of the bed. "Virginia, once a week won't kill you. I'm not kidding."

"Of *course*, Sweetie. If that's what you *want*. I mean."

The young man stood up suddenly.

"Will you tell Cook I'm ready for breakfast?" he asked, starting to leave for somewhere.

"Give us a teeny *kiss* first," she said. "You ole soldier boy."

He bent over and kissed her wonderful mouth and left the room.

He climbed a flight of wide, thickly carpeted steps, and at the top landing turned to his left. He rapped twice at the second door, on the outside of which was tacked a white, formal card from the old Waldorf Astoria Hotel in New York: *Please Do Not Disturb*. There was a faded notation in ink, written in the margin of the card:

Going to Liberty Bond rally. Be back. Meet Tom for me in lobby at six. His left shoulder is higher than his right and he smokes a darling little pipe. Love, Me.

The note was written to the young man's mother, and he had read it when he was a small boy, and a hundred times since, and he read it now: in March, 1944.

"Come in, come in!" called a busy voice. And the young man entered.

By the window, a very nice-looking woman in her early fifties sat at a fold-leg card table. She wore a charming beige

morning gown, and on her feet a pair of extremely dirty white gym shoes. "Well, Dickie Camson," she said. "How did you ever get up so early, you lazy boy?"

"One of those things," said the young man, smiling easily. He kissed her on the cheek, and with one hand on the back of her chair casually examined the huge leather-bound book opened before her. "How's the collection coming?" he asked.

"Lovely. Simply lovely. "*This* book—you haven't seen it, you terrible boy—is brand new. Billy and Cook are going to save me all theirs, and you can save me all *yours*."

"Just cancelled American two-cent stamps, eh?" said the young man.

"Quite an idea." He looked around the room. "How's the radio going?"

It was tuned to the same station he had had on downstairs.

"Lovely. I took the exercises this morning."

"Now, Aunt Rena, I asked you to stop taking those crazy exercises. I mean you'll strain yourself. I mean there's no sense to it."

"I like them," said his aunt firmly, turning a page in her album. "I like the music they play with them. All the old tunes. And it certainly doesn't seem fair to listen to the music and not take the exercises."

"It *is* fair. Now please cut it out. A little less integrity," her nephew said. He walked around the room a bit, then sat

down heavily on the window seat. He looked out across the park, searching between the trees for the way to tell her that he was leaving. He had wanted her to be the one woman in 1944 who did not have someone's hourglass to watch. Now he knew he had to give her his. A gift to the woman in the dirty white gym shoes. The woman with the cancelled American two-cent stamp collection. The woman who was his mother's sister, who had written notes to her in the margins of old Waldorf *Please Do Not Disturb* cards….Must she be told? Must she have his absurd, shiny little hourglass to watch?

"You look just like your mother when you do that with your forehead. Yes. Just like her. Do you remember her at all, Richard?"

"Yes." He took his time. "She never used to walk. She always ran, and then she'd stop short in a room. And she always used to whistle through her teeth when she was drawing the blinds in my room. The same tune most of the time. It was always with me when I was a boy, but I forgot it as I got older. Then in college—I had a roommate from Memphis, and he was playing some old phonograph records one afternoon, some Bessie Smiths, some Tea Gardens, and one of the numbers nearly knocked me out. It was the tune Mother used to whistle through her teeth, all right. It was called 'I Can't Behave on Sundays 'Cause I'm Bad Seven Days

a Week.' A guy named Altrievi stepped on it when he was tight later on in the term, and I've never heard it since." He stopped. "That's about all I remember. Just dumb stuff."

"Do you remember how she looked?"

"No."

"She was quite a package." His aunt placed her chin in the cup of one of her thin, elegant hands. "Your father couldn't sit still, like a human being, in a room if your mother had left it. He'd just nod idiotically when someone talked to him, keeping those peculiar little eyes of his on the door she'd left by. He was a strange, rather rude little man. He did nothing with interest except make money and stare at your mother. And take your mother sailing in that weird boat he bought. He used to wear a funny little English sailor hat. He said it was his father's. Your mother used to hide it on the days she had to go sailing."

"It was all they found, wasn't it?" asked the young man. "That hat."

But his aunt's glance had fallen on her album page.

"Oh, here's a *beauty*," she said, and she held one of her stamps up to the daylight. "He has such a strong, bashed-nose face. Washington."

The young man got up from the window seat. "Virginia told Cook to fix breakfast. I'd better go downstairs," he said. But instead of leaving he walked over to his aunt's card table.

"Aunt Rena," he said, "give me your attention a minute."

His aunt's intelligent face turned up to him.

"Aunt—Uh—There's a war on. Uh—I mean you've seen it in the newsreels. I mean you've heard it on the radio and all, haven't you?"

"Certainly," she snorted.

"Well, I'm going. I have to go. I'm leaving this morning."

"I knew you'd have to," said his aunt, without panic, without bitter-sentimental reference to "the last one." She was wonderful, he thought. She was the sanest woman in the world.

The young man stood up, setting his hourglass flippantly on the table—the only way to do it. "Virginia'll come to see you a lot, Kiddo," he told her. "And she'll take you to the movies pretty often. There's an old W.C. Fields picture coming to the Sutton next week. You like Fields."

His aunt stood up, too, but moved briskly past him. "I have a letter of introduction for you," she announced. "To a friend of mine."

She was over at her writing desk now. She opened the topmost left-hand drawer, positively, and took out a white envelope. Then she went back to her stamp-album table again and casually handed the envelope to her nephew. "I didn't seal it," she said, "and you can read it if you like."

The young man looked at the envelope in his hand. It

was addressed in his aunt's rather strong handwriting to a Lieutenant Thomas E. Cleve, Jr.

"He's a wonderful young man," said his aunt. "He's with the Sixty-Ninth. He'll look after you, I'm not at all worried." She added impressively, "I *knew* this would happen two years ago, and immediately I thought of Tommy. He'll be marvelously considerate of you." She turned around, rather vaguely this time, and walked less briskly back to her writing desk. Again she opened a drawer. She took out a large, framed photograph of a young man in the high-collared, 1917 uniform of a second lieutenant.

She moved unsteadily back to her nephew, holding the picture out for him to see. "This is his picture," she informed him. "This is Tom Cleve's picture."

"I have to go now, Aunt," the young man said. "Good-by. You won't need anything. I mean you won't need anything. I'll write to you."

"Good-by, my dear, dear boy," his aunt said, kissing him.

"You find Tom Cleve now. He'll look after you, till you get settled and all."

"Yes. Good-by."

His aunt said absently, "Good-by, my darling boy."

"Good-by." He left the room and nearly stumbled down the stairs.

At the lower landing he took the envelope, tore it in

halves, quarters, then eighths. He didn't seem to know what to do with the wad, so he jammed it into his trouser pocket.

"Sweetie. *Everything's* cold. Your eggs and all."

"You can take her to the movies once a week," he said. "It won't kill you."

"Who said it *would*? Did I ever once say it would?"

"No." He walked into the dining room.

Other Books From
Devault-Graves Digital Editions